# My First Book Of Patterns
## Capital Letters

With Animal Coloring and Activity Pages

Wonder House

# A for Alligator

Color the Letter **A** and the **ALLIGATOR** brightly.

**A**

**Alligator**

Trace the Letter.

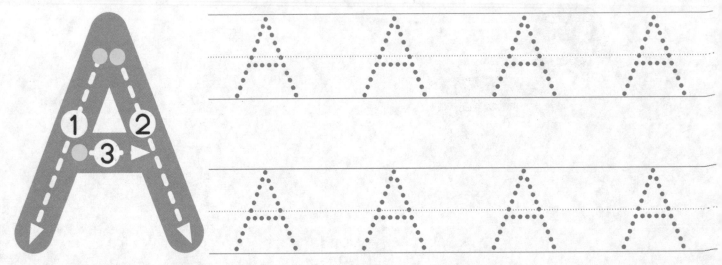

# B for Bear

Color the Letter **B** and the **BEAR** brightly.

B

**Bear**

Trace the Letter.

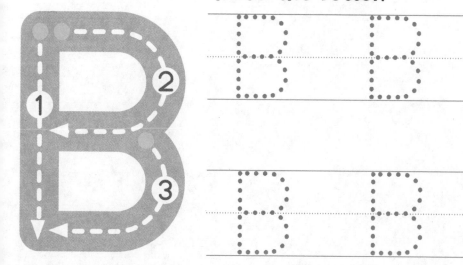

B B B B

B B B B

# C for Cat

Color the Letter C and the CAT brightly.

Cat

Trace the Letter.

# D for Dog

Color the Letter D and the DOG brightly.

Dog

Trace the Letter.

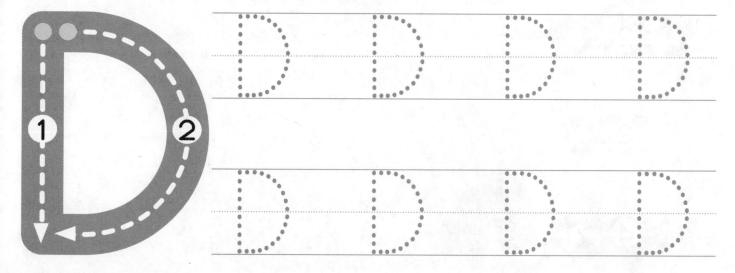

# E for Elephant

Color the letter **E** and the **ELEPHANT** brightly.

**Elephant**

## Trace the Letter.

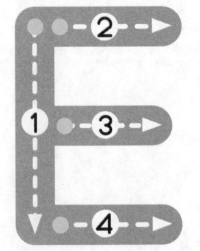

# Find the First Letter!

Circle the beginning letter of each picture.

E A B

C E B

D A E

A D C

# Draw a Circle around the pictures whose name begins with the given letter.

# Draw a line from each letter to the picture whose name begins with that letter.

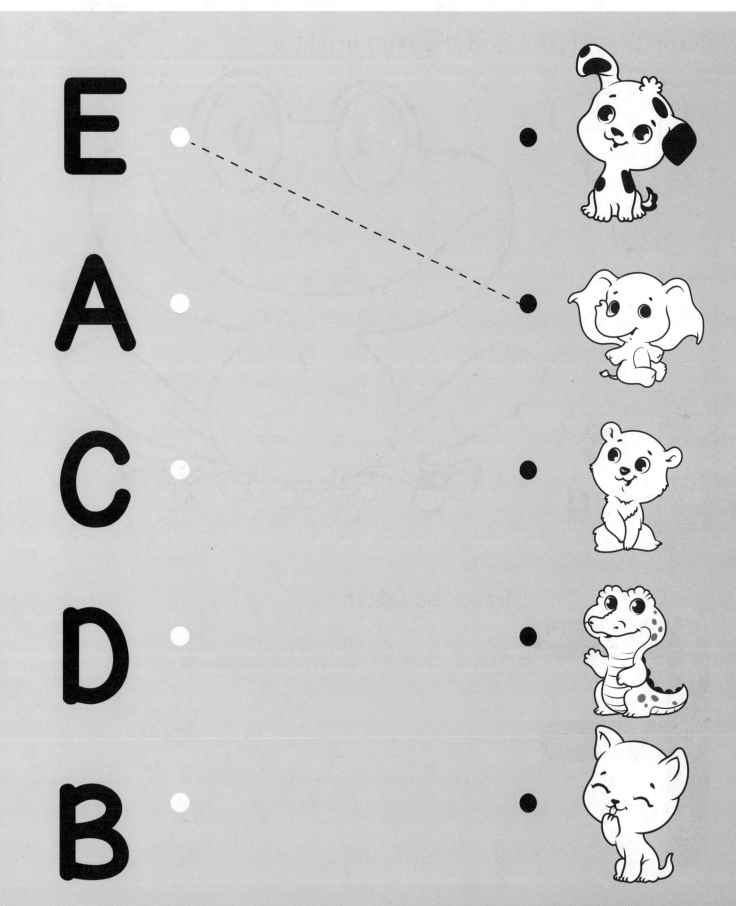

# F for Frog

Color the letter f and the FROG brightly.

F

Frog

Trace the letter.

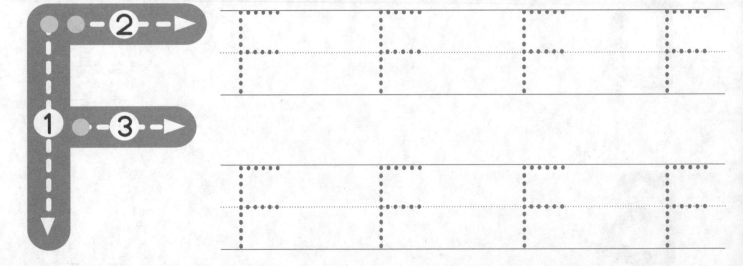

# G for Giraffe

Color the Letter G and the GIRAFFE brightly.

**Giraffe**

Trace the Letter.

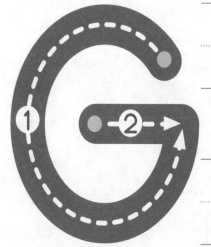

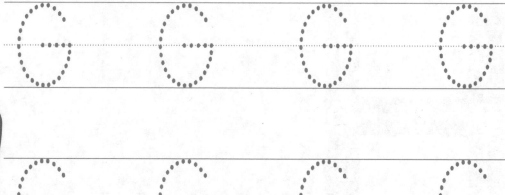

# H for Horse

Color the letter H and the HORSE brightly.

Horse

Trace the Letter.

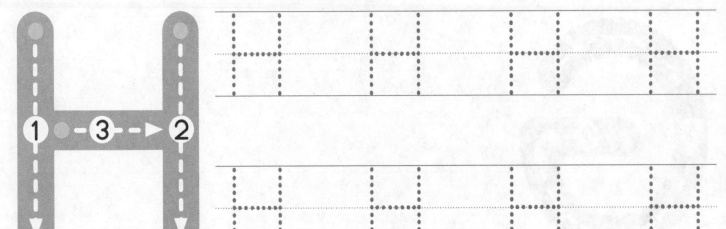

# I for Iguana

Color the Letter I and the IGUANA brightly.

**I**

**Iguana**

Trace the Letter.

2 → 1 → 3 →

# J for Jellyfish

Color the letter J and the JELLYFISH brightly.

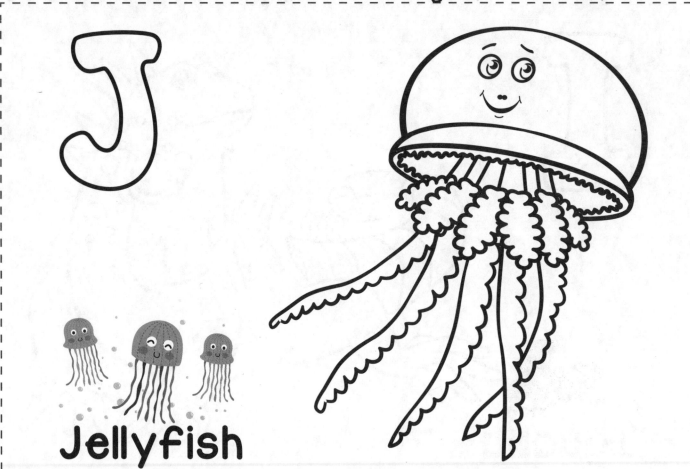

J

Jellyfish

Trace the Letter.

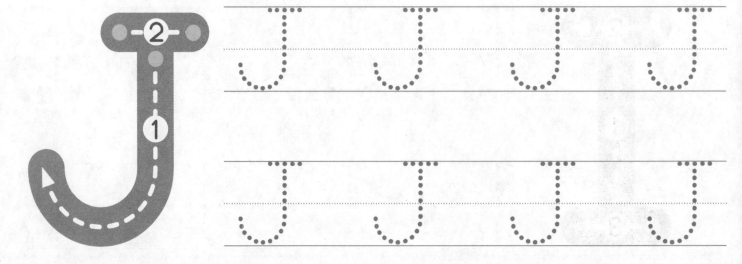

# Find the First Letter!

Circle the beginning Letter of each picture.

G   J   I

F   H   G

I   G   J

H   J   G

# Draw a Circle around the pictures whose name begins with the given letter.

# Draw a line from each letter to the picture whose name begins with that letter.

# K for Koala

Color the Letter K and the KOALA brightly.

**Koala**

Trace the Letter.

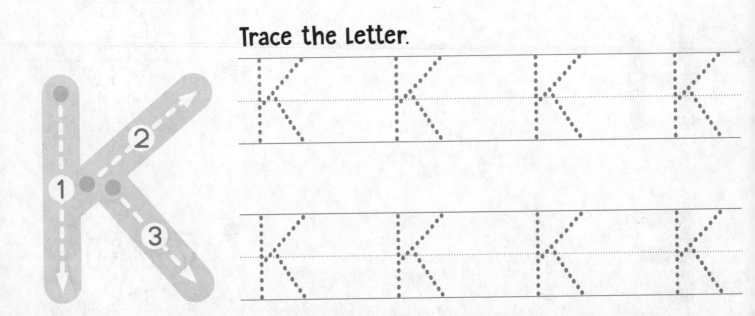

# L for Lion

Color the Letter L and the LION brightly.

Lion

Trace the Letter.

# M for Monkey

Color the Letter **M** and the **MONKEY** brightly.

Monkey

Trace the Letter.

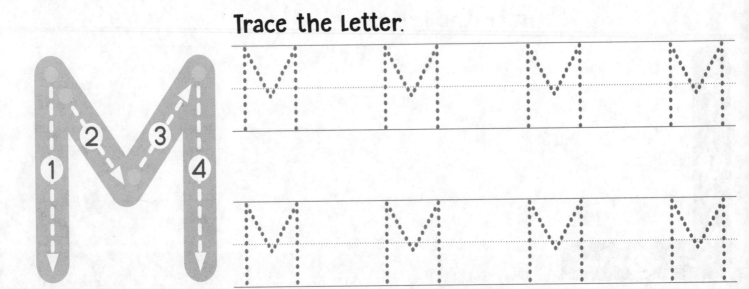

# N for Nightingale

Color the Letter **N** and the **NIGHTINGALE** brightly.

**Nightingale**

Trace the Letter.

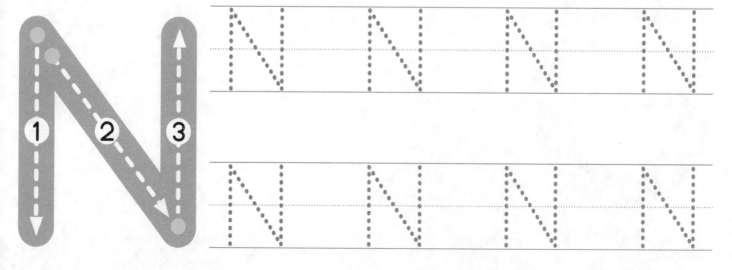

# O for Owl

Color the Letter O and the OWL brightly.

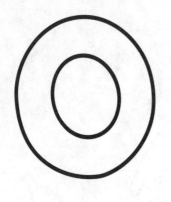

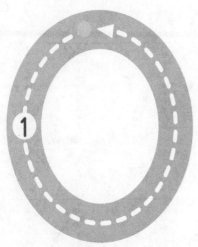

Owl

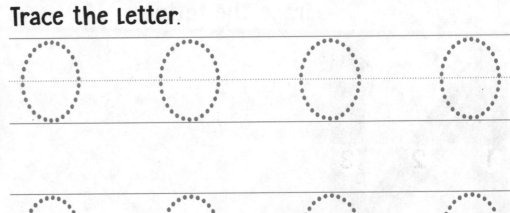

1

Trace the Letter.

O O O O

O O O O

# Find the First Letter!
## Circle the beginning letter of each picture.

K M O

L N M

N M O

N L K

# Draw a Circle around the pictures whose name begins with the given letter.

# Draw a line from each letter to the picture whose name begins with that letter.

# p for Parrot

Color the letter P and the PARROT brightly.

P

Parrot

Trace the Letter.

P   P   P   P

P   P   P   P

# Q for Queen Bee

Color the Letter Q and the QUEEN BEE brightly.

Queen Bee

Trace the Letter.

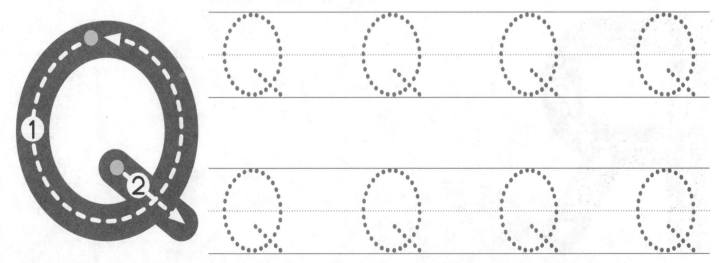

# R for Rhinoceros

Color the Letter R and the RHINOCEROS brightly.

**R**

Rhinoceros

Trace the Letter.

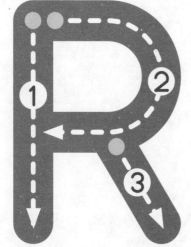

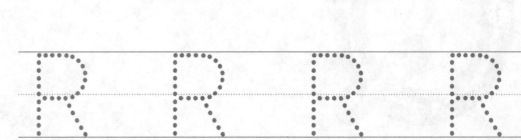

R R R R

R R R R

# S for Squirrel

Color the Letter S and the SQUIRREL brightly.

S

Squirrel

Trace the Letter.

S

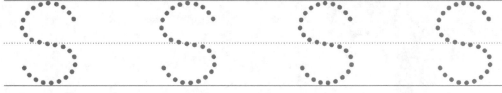

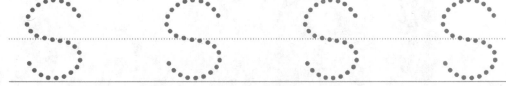

# T for Tortoise

Color the Letter T and the TORTOISE brightly.

Tortoise

Trace the Letter.

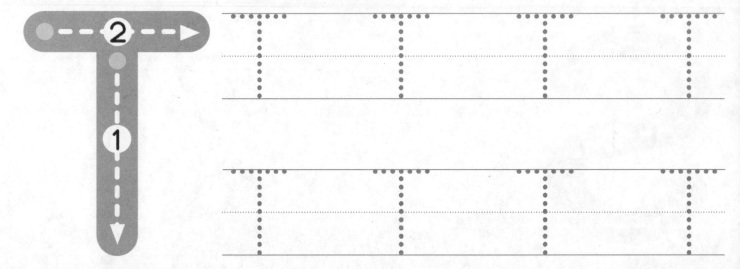

# Find the First Letter!

Circle the beginning letter of each picture.

P R S

Q S R

T R S

S P Q

# Draw a Circle around the pictures whose name begins with the given letter.

# Draw a line from each letter to the picture whose name begins with that letter.

P

Q

R

S

T

# U for Unicorn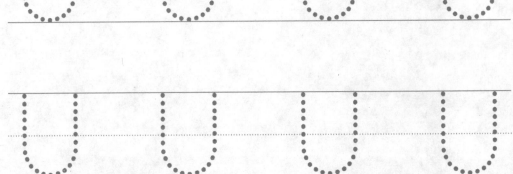

Color the Letter U and the UNICORN brightly.

Unicorn

Trace the Letter.

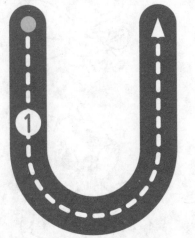

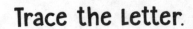

# V for Vulture

Color the Letter V and the VULTURE brightly.

Vulture

Trace the Letter.

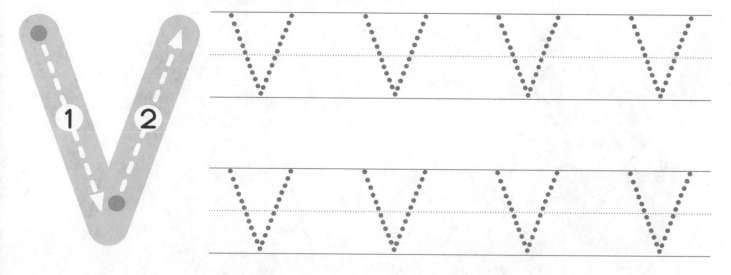

# W for Whale

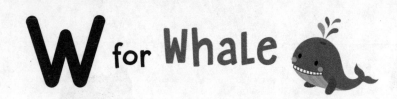

Color the letter W and the WHALE brightly.

Whale

Trace the Letter.

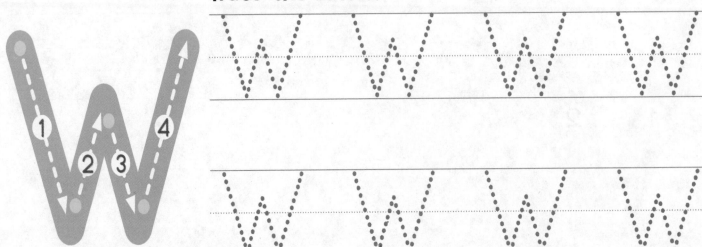

# X for X-ray fish

Color the letter X and the X-RAY FISH brightly.

X-ray fish

Trace the Letter.

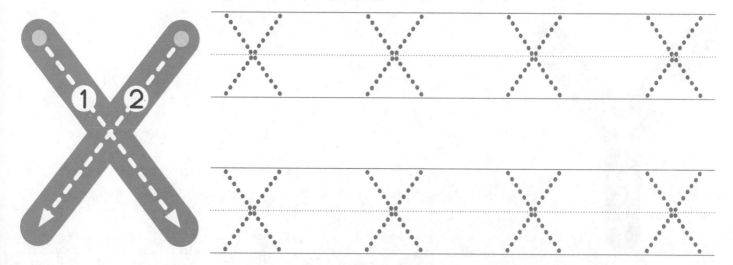

# Y for Yak

## Color the Letter Y and the YAK brightly.

Yak

## Trace the Letter.

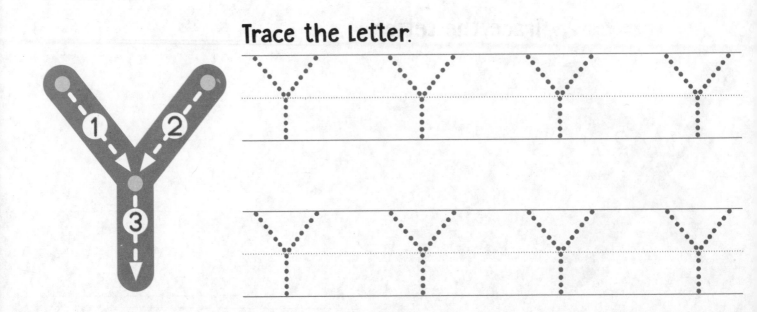

# Z for Zebra

Color the Letter Z and the ZEBRA brightly.

Z

Zebra

Trace the Letter.

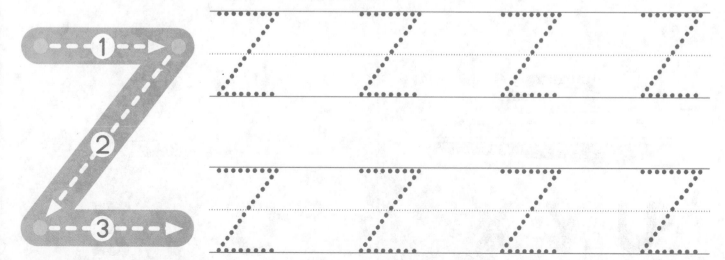

# Find the First Letter!
Circle the beginning Letter of each picture.

U W Y

V Z Y

W X Y

X U V

U Y X

U V Z

# Draw a line from each letter to the picture whose name begins with that letter.

# Draw a Circle around the pictures whose name begins with that letter.

# Write the missing letters of each word.

 _NT

 C_NDL_

 A___IGATOR

 _ARN

 _AN

 PE_C_L

 E_G

 _O_KE_

 _E_RA

 _A_P

 _AM

 __ANGE

# Letter Puzzle
Write the missing letters of each word.

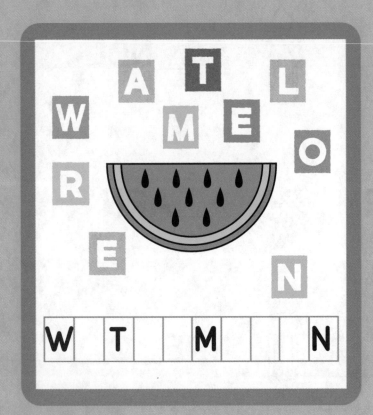

W A T E L
M E
W R O
R
E N

| W | | T | | M | | N |

A P E
E
P L

| A | | | | E |

T T O R
O
A R
C

| | R | | C | | R |

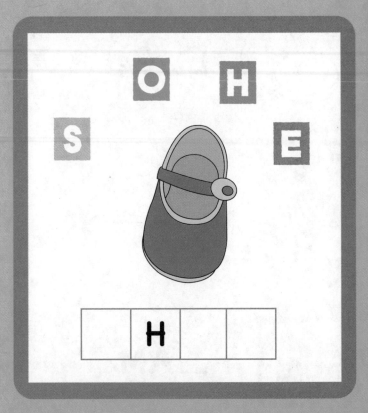

O H
S E

| | H | |

# Fill in the Missing Letters.

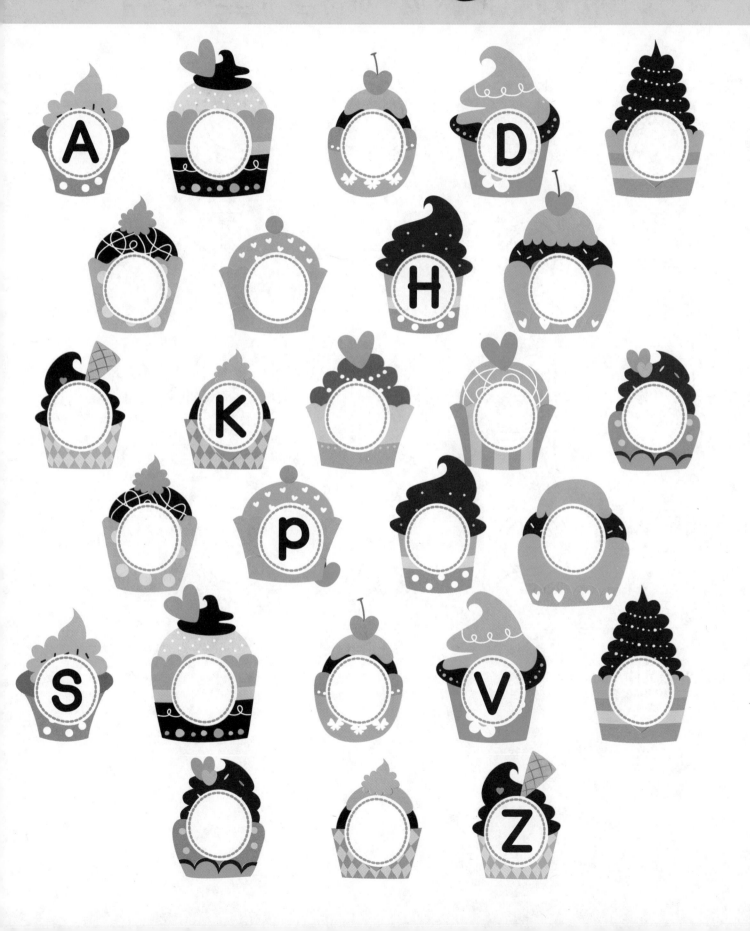

# TRACE

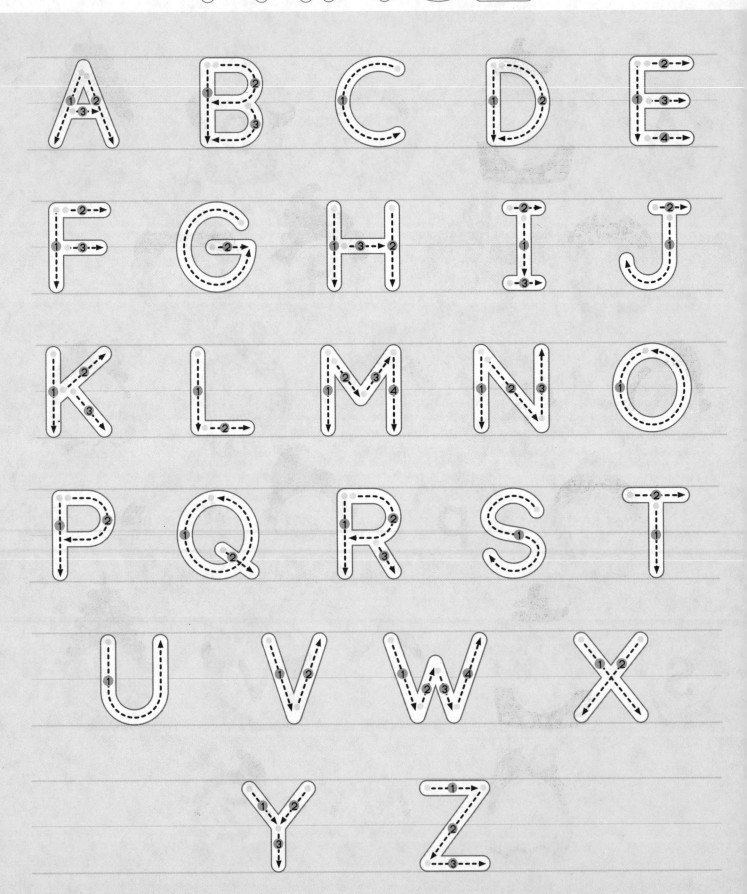

# ANSWERS

### Find the First Letter!
Circle the beginning Letter for each picture.

E Ⓐ B     C E Ⓑ

Ⓓ A E     A D Ⓒ

### Draw a Circle around the pictures whose name begins with that letter.

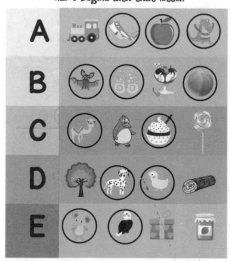

### Draw a line from each letter to the picture whose name begins with that letter.

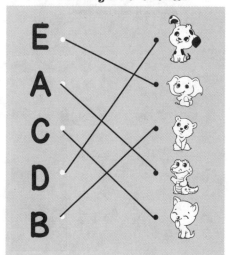

### Find the First Letter!
Circle the beginning Letter for each picture.

Ⓖ J I     F Ⓗ G

Ⓘ G J     H Ⓙ G

### Draw a Circle around the pictures whose name begins with that letter.

### Draw a line from each letter to the picture whose name begins with that letter.

### Find the First Letter!
Circle the beginning Letter for each picture.

Ⓚ M O     Ⓛ N M

Ⓝ M O     N L Ⓚ

### Draw a Circle around the pictures whose name begins with that letter.

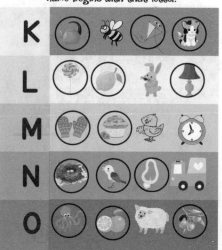

### Draw a line from each letter to the picture whose name begins with that letter.

# ANSWERS

### Find the First Letter!
Circle the beginning Letter for each picture.

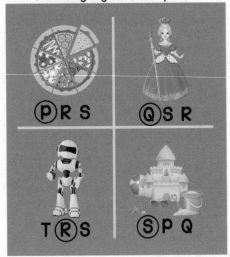

P **R** S          **Q** S R

T **R** S          **S** P Q

### Draw a Circle around the pictures whose name begins with that letter.

### Draw a line from each letter to the picture whose name begins with that letter.

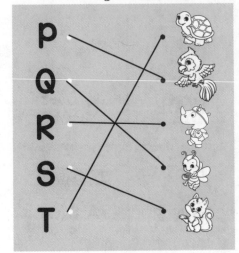

### Find the First Letter!
Circle the beginning Letter for each picture.

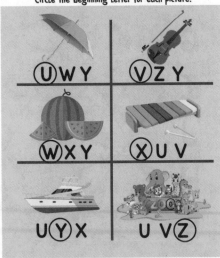

**U** W Y          **V** Z Y

**W** X Y          **X** U V

U **Y** X          U V **Z**

### Draw a line from each letter to the picture whose name begins with that letter.

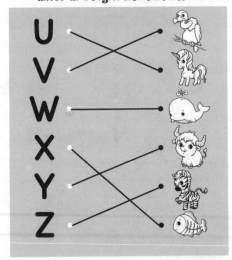

### Draw a Circle around the pictures whose name begins with that letter.

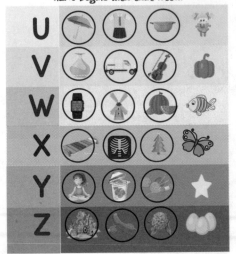

### Write the missing letters of each word.

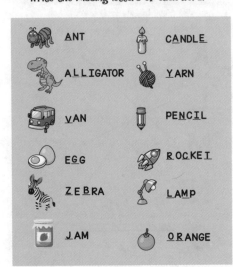

ANT          C_A_NDLE

_A_LLIGATOR          _Y_ARN

_V_AN          PENCIL

_E_GG          _R_OCKE_T_

_Z_EBRA          _L_AMP

_J_AM          _O_RANGE

### Write the missing letters of each word.

WATERMELON          APPLE

TRACTOR          SHOE

### Fill in the Missing Letters.

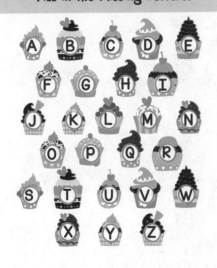